# A Naked Lie

AND OTHER STORIES

# A Naked Lie

AND OTHER STORIES

Nemen M. Kpahn

Village Tales Publishing
LAWRENCVILLE, GA

A catalog record for this book is available from the Library of Congress:
LCCN: 2019912843
ISBN: 9781945408526
eISBN: 9781945408533

Published By:
Village Tales Publishing
Lawrenceville, GA

www.villagetalespublishing.com
www.oass.villagetalespublishing.com

Book Layout by OASS
Cover Photo: Downtown Monrovia Erik (HASH) Hershman

Printed in the United States

# Dedication

*This book is dedicated to my brother,*

*Sam Gonkerwon Kpahn*

---

*"War means fighting, and fighting means killing."*
Nathan Bedford Forrest

*"Civil wars leave nothing but tombs."*
Alphonse De Lamartine

*"War demands sacrifice of the people.*
*It gives only suffering in return."*
Frederic Clemson Howe

# Contents

# Introduction

Based on actual events, these fictitious short stories are set in postwar Liberia following the end of the civil war.

**A Naked Lie** - The liar spoke with assurance, using common knowledge to slide the lie right in. God forbid, had it been during wartime, the accused would have died. During the civil war, many Liberians became victims because of lies. People can sometimes go to the extreme to prove their beliefs no matter what; even uncaring of the pain they could cause others.

**All That Matters** tells the story of the overly ambitious self-made man, Garretson Biah, and the futility of the Liberian elections. Biah desired so much to become an honorable member of the House of Representatives that his fiery ambition led to his downfall; mostly due to unethical personalities with little or no substance.

**Jean Pierre and Kpormor** is a mysterious tale of the falling apart of two very good friends, and the tragic consequences of such falling out when not properly addressed.

In the settlement along the fertile banks of the St. Paul River, **Old But Not Cold** is an unconventional love story between an alcoholic old man whose life had dealt cruel blows of experiments and surprises, and a jilted young woman whose unfaithful boyfriend constantly breaks her heart. Respect existence or expect resistance; the coming together of two seemingly different people shows love can strike in the least expected way to the least expected people.

**Sea Breeze** is set in postwar Liberia when a young man succumbed to the temptations of armed robbery, and the young woman who loved his despicable characters, irrespective of being in harm's way.

**We Will Remember Them** – In 1990, a group of armed men, members of the Armed Forces of Liberia, stormed the Lutheran Church in Sinkor, killing untold numbers of unarmed civilians. The effect one of Liberia's most notorious massacres had on one family is told from Meanyean's memory, a survivor leaving Liberia for good, to live in Australia.

From 1989-2003, the civil war in Liberia dragged on for seven hellacious years, and further displaced thousands of Liberians into refugee camps in neighboring countries and other world communities. Around 250,000 people were killed, while thousands more were mutilated and raped, often by armies of drugged child soldiers led by ruthless warlords. It's aftermath, however, turned out to be longer and more treacherous.

## A NAKED LIE

The liar spoke with assurance, using common knowledge to slide the lie right in. God forbid, had it been during wartime, the accused would have died. During the civil war, many Liberians became victims because of lies. People can sometimes go to the extreme to prove their beliefs no matter what; even uncaring of the pain they could cause others.

---

# A Naked Lie

Liberia had changed a lot from the careful and easy-going life where the cost of living was relatively easy, serving as a magnet for West African immigrants from Ghana, Nigeria, Guinea, and other countries in search of the mighty U.S. dollars which was legal currency in the country. Now the country lay in ruins with an almost nonexistent economy. I had returned to the country of my birth with high hopes to rebuild my life and restore the years of destruction caused by the civil war. Besides, having studied business management and marketing in Accra, Ghana, my Liberian accent made it difficult for me to secure employment. Ghanaians themselves, especially young men, were having a hard time securing employment; what more about a foreigner like me.

In Liberia, I was sure the situation would be relatively easy. On one of the overcrowded buses that ferried people from one place to another in this relatively once prosperous West African country, I remembered a middle-aged lady asking me how long had it been since I was last in Liberia.

"Eight years," I replied in a smug voice.

"My brother, Liberia is hard now o," she said. "It's not like before. The Sweet Land of Liberty is now a bitter land. You have to struggle to make ends meet."

That was not the sort of message I wanted to hear. Surely my fellow passenger was exaggerating. It's been merely three months since my return to this overcrowded city. The old infrastructures seemed to serve as a magnet to the poor and destitute.

I took a cold-water bath using a bucket and hurried to New Georgia Estate junction to get on one of those crowded mini-buses that took commuters to and from the city. The narrow two-lane road leading to the city, pot-holed by rocket shells landing on its surface during the dark days, remained unchanged. Monrovians were fond of reminding Johnny-just-come, like me, that government officials were too busy attending conferences in far-flung corners of the globe, from Jakarta to San Francisco, to help "Liberia regain her international image," than to pay attention to repairing basic infrastructure. Funny whenever these senior government officials returned from those international conferences, and you ask them what was the result of their trip, the answer was invariably the same; "fruitful and rewarding." But they would never explain what was fruitful about the latest trip to Lilongwe, apart from the per diem they received.

My optimism after attending numerous job interviews had dimmed. But one cannot sit down and give up, or succumb to the temptation and scourge of drugs. So here I was, dressed in ironed cotton trousers and a monogram white shirt, prepare to fight for a seat on a commuter bus. The carboy[1] leaped out of the still-moving vehicle. Those of us waiting to take the place of the single passenger exiting the bus pressed forward to the side entrance, almost blocking the path of the lady getting off.

"My people, y'all give me chance to get down now," she pleaded.

A thick, muscular fellow elbowed me out of contention and jumped into the vehicle. I cursed under my breath as the bus drove off. I stood waiting for the next chance, while there was no orderly line or a specific bus stop sign. Drivers simply pickup, and drop off passengers anywhere along the dusty road. Peddlers, scurrying to do business with passing motorists, crammed the roadside. The congestion irritated me. Accra was just as chaotic as Monrovia. However, it was a lot more orderly and developed compared to this city.

----

1 Gatekeeper of commercial buses who collects passengers' fares.

I got here at 7:30 a.m. and it was already 8 a.m. My interview was slated for 9 a.m. I was beginning to worry. I did not want to be late for my interview although under the best of conditions the trip to central Monrovia should be around 10 minutes. Now it took between 30 minutes to an hour, depending on the traffic.

My portfolio bag seemed to be a hindrance. Every time I tried to squeeze my way into a bus, the edge of the bag somehow managed to become entangled in the door, and then someone would beat me to the vacant seat. Come hell or hot water, I was going to get on the green bus approaching us. As soon as the bus came to a stop, I elbowed an elderly lady out of the way and made my way to a vacant seat. Now seated, I pondered on what I just did. The city made one selfish and uncaring at times, oblivious to the norms which we grew up with, such as respect for the elderly.

These bus rides are lively. Liberians waste no time in starting a conversation, sometimes the most intimate types that are shared among close friends. They carry on these conversations with strangers without a hint of embarrassment. UNMIL radio station, ever-popular with bus drivers, played in the background as passengers debated whether people accused of war crimes should be banned from the upcoming elections. They could be elected leaders for a new Liberia, both for the legislature (parliament) and the presidency. I tried to focus on my pending interview, doing my best to ignore the hearty conversation going on around me.

A big man with broad nose and thick biceps looked directly at me and asked, "Young man, know one thing I like?"

His physical form marked him as someone who did hard labor jobs. Before I would answer, he said, "President Lassana Conteh of Guinea, ah . . . I like that man. He says any town or region that allows rebels to come to their area, he would waste no time. He will bring his airplanes, helicopters, and war tanks and make sure he bomb that area. He will destroy both the rebels and the people who allowed the rebels to come into that town."

'Because the man doesn't waste time with rebels, there are no rebels in Guinea?' I tried to follow his logic. His thick Guinean accent was hard to follow.

"Da true," a woman said in Liberian koloqua English. Dressed in a colorful lappa[2] suit, and wearing a bag on her shoulders, suggested she was a market woman.

From my experience, the way the man addressed the issue of rebel infiltration raised concerned. Against my better judgment, I said, "My brother, what you said puzzled me. Are you saying that if rebels enter a town, the government can kill everyone in that town, even if they are civilians?"

"My brother, don't ask me that kind of question," he said. "Where are you coming from? You don't know how bad rebels are? From the time

---

2 A long skirt-wrapper women wear

rebels enter Liberia and Sierra Leone, look at the way the two countries are. No development . . . children killing parents, people smoking and doing bad things to each other. Rebel business is not a good thing for anyone to support."

I did not say anything.

"My brother, do you support rebel business," he asked, pointing directly at me.

"Of course not," I replied. "I do not support rebel business."

"Then, why are you against President Conteh's plan to kill rebels?"

"I am not against a government soldier killing an armed rebel combatant who wants to kill him as well," I said. "What I am against is the killing of innocent civilians without the government making efforts to ensure their safety. Innocent people die in every war, but at least efforts should be made to avoid killing civilians."

Before he would say anything, I continued.

"When rebels enter a town, they do not ask permission from the town's people. I remembered when we were living in Danane, and the rebels invaded the town, they came on a market day, Thursday, November 29, 2002. Children had gone to school and their parents had gone to work. Some of us had simply gone to the market as it was market day. Suddenly, we heard the sounds of gunshots coming from all directions. Rockets were falling and everyone ran helter-skelter for dear life, including the soldiers. Within the space of two hours, the rebels were in full control of the town, breaking into the prison and

freeing prisoners, arresting local government officials and looting. What opportunity did we, the
civilians without guns, have to tell the rebels that
we did not want them in our town?"

The anti-rebel vigilante stared as if stunned
by my frank personal testimony.

"Look at this rebel," he screamed, pointing at
me.

My brain stuttered for a moment. My eyes
took in more light than I expected. Every part of
me went on pause while my thoughts caught up.
Before I could say anything, he went on.

"Eh you don't think I remember you, old rebel," he said. "You are, C.O. Kill Me Quick. My people, who do not know this man?" he asked, looking around the bus. "This is C.O. Kill Me Quick.
During the war, when this man," he pointed at
me, "says, 'Your own finish today,' my brother .
.. my sister, just know that your life is finished
on that day. This man was the commander of the
rebels when they captured Harbel[3]. I remember
the day when they invaded Harbel in 1996 . . .
this man was leading his troops into Firestone
Duside Hospital. He was wearing a red shirt with
cowries shells on a string tied around his neck.
He had three magazines in his gun, which he tied
together with scotch tape." He looked at me and
asked, "You do remember that day, right?"

Too shocked to speak, I kept my silence. But
my silence only gave him momentum to carry on
with his rhetoric.

_______________

3 Town in Margibi County, Liberia.

"I saw you moving from bed to bed, killing sick patients in the hospital," the man continued. "My people," he screamed, lifting his hands, beating his chest, and knocking his thighs in a dramatic affirmation of the truth. His gestures were more eloquent than his words.

"This man is a wicked man," he screamed. "He was chopping and shooting people, left, and right. Do you remembered when you reached my bed and wanted to shoot me," he asked, looking directly at me. "Thankfully, I had $100 US dollars on me, which I gave you . . . pleading for my life. You told me to get the hell out of the hospital."

He turned his attention to the passengers.

"My people, God didn't want me to die that day," he continued. "I know God kept me alive for a reason. C. O. Kill Me Quick could have shot me and still take the money. Instead, God held his hand."

Everyone was staring at me with narrowed eyes now; rigid, cold, and hard. Those angry eyes were their untold pain. Everyone in this country, young as well as old, had experienced trauma and atrocities. My heart hammered erratically in my chest.

"These damn rebel leaders who kill our people . . . mixing among us and behaving like normal human beings," one twenty-something-year-old woman said, cutting her eyes. "I see why he was against government troops attacking rebels."

I found my voice and asked my accuser, "What year . . . and month, did I, C.O. Kill Me

Quick, attacked the Duside hospital, where you were sick?"

"Don't act like you don't know the date and time," he said. His facial expression was one of absolute disdain. "You know, C.O. Kill Me Quick. Don't act as if you're innocent before these people."

"I asked you a simple question," I said, and repeated, "What month . . . and what year, did I and my men attacked the Duside hospital?"

"That's a stupid question," he said, with a face of utter nonchalance, as if he were merely having a casual conversation with a friend.

"Answer the man's question," the same young lady demanded.

Everyone's eyes turned on my accuser.

I shifted uncomfortably in my seat. In this post-war country, mob justice was just a stone throw away.

"C.O. Kill Me Quick, you and your men attacked Duside Hospital in December 1990," he said, emphatically and authentically.

"Your lies have finally caught up with you," I said to him, "because in December 1990, I was not in this country. I ran away from the country on August 1990, on a merchant vessel called the Bulk Challenge. We landed in Buduburam Refugee Camp. In December 1990, I was attending a business school in Ghana called, the institute of Management Studies."

"You are a liar," my accuser bellowed. "I have never seen somebody who can lie like this."

"I am not as great a liar and actor like you," I replied. "My people, please listen. In 1990, I was a student at the Institute of Management Studies in Accra. Here is my student I.D. Card from the school with the year on it." I pulled out the I.D. and handed it to the man sitting beside me.

He inspected the I.D. card which had the dates I attended, from 1990-1993. Then, I pulled out my transcript and handed it to another passenger, who inspected it right away. I had studied commencing from November 1990 to October 1993. Fellow passengers murmured as the two strangers were confirming the facts of my whereabouts.

"This man is lying," my accuser insisted. "I know him. I saw him in Duside Hospital. He's lying about his book business."

At best, my accuser was attempting to stoke the common animosity of most common Liberians who resented the air of intellectual superiority exhibited by the elites towards the common people.

"Shut your damn mouth," a man dressed in military bearing shouted. He was seated at the back of the bus. "Do you realize what you've done? Had it been wartime, what you've accused this man of, he would have been killed. Killed for no reason. Your fabrication was believable, that even I, and I'm sure, others, believed you. The papers clearly show that he was in Ghana during the time you accused him of killing at Duside Hospital."

My accuser said nothing.

"Are you suggesting that during the peak of the 1990 war, this man, who escaped the hell-hole called, Liberia, started school in Ghana and somehow managed to come back to Liberia to become a rebel chief," the soldier continued. "For argument sake, even if he wanted to, how could he have gotten back? There were no transportations coming back to Liberia."

"Driver, stop the bus," another passenger screamed. "Stop . . . let this criminal out," she pointed at my accuser.

"Madam, I can't," the driver said. "The man paid his fare. I will let him out when we get into the city."

"Stop the car! Stop the car!" Passengers chanted. "Put the man down!"

The driver stopped the bus and asked my accuser to get off. He did, and without a fight.

I thought it worthwhile to explain to my fellow passengers that I had recently returned to Liberia now that there was peace to rebuild my life like them. I explained that the reason I had my school documents with me was that I was headed for a job interview. My accuser had not just lied; he had uttered a naked lie.

I reached my destination and step out of the bus on Johnson Street, pondering the incident. Without further ado, I headed to my job interview.

## ALL THAT MATTERS

The story of an overly ambitious self-made man, Garretson Biah, and the futility of the Liberian elections. Biah desired so much to become an honorable member of the House of Representatives that his fiery ambition led to his downfall; mostly due to unethical personalities with little or no substance.

# All That Matters

The sun was shining brightly over the town of Zuolay, in Lower Nimba County, along the main dusty highway between Ganta and Tappeta. The long rainy season that transformed the road in the district into a thick layer of slippery mud and grime had ended. For the past weeks, one thing remained paramount in the minds of the people of electoral District 9 that connected them with their kinsmen in surrounding towns and villages; the exercise called, democracy. Every 6 years the ritual started all over. Every house along the main road, and the side road leading to Zuolay's main street comprising of a cluster of shops, were decorated back to back with pictures of a dozen or more sons and daughters of the district in large color pictures all announcing the same things for the voters: better schools, good roads, jobs, and developments in copious amount.

There was little in terms of ideology, or policies, that differentiated the ambitious candidates vying for the position of member of the House of Representatives from the other. The eclectic mix of personalities and the surplus of political parties focused more on personalities than substance. The elections were more about jobs and the trappings of power.

Often seen were the mandatory large sports utility vehicles like Toyota Land Cruisers, or the ubiquitous Nissan Pathfinders, or Nissan Patrols, and the entourage of followers, some to tote the Honorable's bag and his mineral water bottle, or drive his car. Of course, there were free recharge scratch phone cards, free gasoline slips and per diems for sitting in parliament for only six months of the year. The position, however, came with a lot of responsibilities and expectations; a mother giving birth expected all of her medical bills to be paid by the Honorable although she was neither the partner nor a relative of the member of the House. A man who died in Monrovia, his family back in the electoral expected the Representative to pay for the repatriation and burial of the deceased in his home village in Gblonar, or Zoetuo. Every birthday celebrant expected the Honorable to contribute towards the celebration, along with honoring countless invitations to school closing programs.

Whatever the drawbacks, the position and prestige of being a Representative were too great to ignore. Yarmie Saye, a youngish man with a thin mustache and round eyes, came from Minnesota in the American Mid-west to contest on the ticket of one of the surpluses of political parties. The daughter of a former Representative, Dorcas Johnson, who was a teacher in Monrovia, suddenly got a revelation to represent her people and entered the race. Weamie, a popular barrister from Ziah New Town, also would run. But the main contest was between the incumbent Representative, Ricks Gonkarnue, and Garretson Biah, a popular businessman. Representative Gonkarnue hailed from a prominent royal family from Toweh Town. He had all the power of incumbency, especially name recognition. Most importantly, he had money to fund his campaign. Gonkarnue had the money to pay for airtime on Tappeta FM station as well as the one in Graie.

The Honorable had a group of young men and women on his payroll, predominantly young men, whose job was to put nice pictures of him doing wonderful things for the people of the district; like dedicating a new water hand pump, or donating money to school and clinics on Facebook. Crucially, these young men's job was to upload negative image and gossips about his opponents on social media. It was even rumored that several prominent pastors were on the Honorable payroll, to describe him as a God-fearing leader. Whether these rumors were true or not, no one could say for sure. However, it described how Honorable Gonkarnue had influenced insidious and powerful friends everywhere, from Graie to Toweh Town, from Zuolay to Zeongein, extending as far as Yarwein Clan.

His main opponent, Garretson Biah, a rambunctious self-made businessman, seemed determined to win. Back in the days, Garretson started as a bag boy for Sekou Bamballi, the legendary produce seller known in all the towns of Lower Nimba. It was Bamballi who made local farmers money in ripe beans that dotted the entrance to their farms and villages, often used as flowers and allowed to rot on the ground. Bamballi walked from village to village, offering to buy cocoa and coffee beans, bringing money to small farmers and becoming very wealthy in the process.

Even though Sekou Bamballi emigrated to the district as a boy, his command of the native languages were poor. Garretson served as an interpreter for the itinerant trader and learned the tricks of the trade, including tying the threads of weighing machine tight so that the pounds registered on the scale was much lesser than the actual amount. When the war years came and Sekou Bamballi moved back north to his country of birth, Garretson step into his shoes. While other businessmen fled to other countries as bands of rebels marauders pillaged the country and reduced it to the dogs, Garretson remained, buying looted items cheaply from the doped-up boys and selling them in neighboring countries.

If Garretson, the businessman, was unscrupulous, his generosity and largess were legendary. A university girl who found herself out of school with no fees could have her fees paid by the generous businessman. A young man who impregnated a girl with no money to pay for baby diapers could have Garretson pay the bills freely with no questions asked. Garretson had the biggest store in Tappeta, a gas station in Zuolay, a rice mill in Volay, and a produce buying store in Zuatuo. So the election was basically between Ricks Gonkarnue, the incumbent, and the popular businessman, Garretson Biah, or so people thought.

Every nook and cranny of the district was filled with campaigners representing the contestants. Motorbikes and cars were hired to take the message of prosperity for the candidates, disguised as developmental messages in the district. When Ricks Gonkarnue killed a cow in Toweh Town, Garretson responded by killing two cows in Zuolay. When Dorcas Johnson gave plain cheap white T-shirts to her supporters, Garretson printed collar T-shirts adorned with his images in full color for distribution among his supporters. Garretson approached politics with the same ruthless passion he endeavored to do his business. He spared no expense. When a man has got enough money to meet his immediate needs, power beckons with irresistible force. A prudent man, Garretson did not go far in formal education, stopping only in the 6th Grade. His lack of education pained the great man and caused resentment in him for educated people. However, the very education he loathed attracted him to educated people. It gave Garretson immense pride to have college graduates work for him.

Garretson woke up early on election day to take a bucket-bath before casting his ballot. He slaughtered two goats so his many teeming supporters can have food for the day. The man was confident of victory. The popular singer, Morris King, had composed a special campaign song for him. This campaign song played on all the community radio stations in the district, day and night, singing Garretson's praises. While his opponents donated to schools, Garretson donated bags of rice by the dozen, thinking the people wanted immediate gratification. After all, many were wearing his T-shirts.

Biah's friends and supporters already referred to him as the Honorable Garretson Biah. By early morning long queues of eager voters formed around the District Commissioner's compound in Zuolay. The story was the same in Graie, Zuaplay, Marlay and everywhere. The Legislative elections were being held the same day as the presidential elections, featuring George Weah, Joseph Boikai, Alexander Cummings and countless of other candidates, too numerous to name vying for the presidency. But it was the representative position which attracted the most attention. While nominally Garretson pledged his loyalty to one of the frontrunners, he cared little about who became president. As far as Garretson was concerned, the next president of Liberia could come from the moon, as long as he was elected as a member of the House of Representatives, representing the people of District 9.

To spice things up a little, a local band played at his modest three-bedroom house in Bahn Quarter near Gogue, the local river. When provisional results started to come in on the night of the election, Garretson had much to smile about. He was leading in Graie, Zuolay, Volay, and Zeongein. His main opponent, the incumbent, Ricks Gonkarnue, appeared to have won in Toweh Town and Marlay, his hometown; which had been expected. Besides those two towns, Ricks Gonkarnue's re-election bid seemed to have flopped. The incumbent had spent all his spare time carousing with his wife and concubines in Ghana, neglecting his constituents.

Shockingly, Dorcas Johnson, a dark horse candidate, who'd launched a small people-to-people grassroots campaign, won the election. While Garretson and Ricks were flouting their wealth and insulting each other with their supporters on radio and town hall meetings without paying attention to the later, Dorcas Johnson, an RN, had built her campaign slowly from the bottom up. Her supporters walked from door to door, reminding people in the district, who had given them a tablet when they had malaria. They were to trust the person who had given them medication on credit when they were sick and had no money to pay. Strategically, Dorcas had conducted a low-key people-to-people campaign, away from the glare of publicity and flamboyancy.

Garretson's intense disappointment gnarled his bones, seeping deep into his soul.

"They took my money, ate my food, and wore my T-shirt, but give their votes to that b-i-t-c-h," Garretson angrily said to his wife.

Garretson bore his disappointment on the inside. He called Dorcas Johnson and congratulated her publicly. Appearing on Tappeta Community Radio flagship program, Issues in the Press, Garretson publicly declared, "The time for campaigning is over. It is time to support our elected Representative and work in the interest of our people. We must move our district forward. In this regard, I am having a feast in Zuolay, and I am inviting our newly elected, Honorable Dorcas Johnson, to this feast for us to smoke a peace pipe."

Garretson Biah was playing the part of a good loser, gracious and magnanimous in defeat. His attitude contrasted sharply with incumbent Representative, Gonkarnue Ricks, who accused the elections as being rigged and unfair, calling for re-election although every other person agreed the election was free, fair, and transparent.

A reconciler by nature and not wanting to be outdone by her defeated opponent, Dorcas Johnson accepted the invitation to go to Zuolay for the much-anticipated feast. There were some in the camp of the newly elected Representative who was a little caution and did not want her to attend the feast. Such voices were few and distant, and quickly shut down by the loud clamoring voices of the vast majority wanting the district to be a shining light, and example to other constituencies in the country.

A feast placed before the guests, tabletops layered with huge pans of the most delicious food and drinks lined the compound, capable of making one's mouth water. A cow, three goats, and some chickens had been slaughtered. Nothing was spared; cane juice, the potent locally distilled gin, palm wine, and imported liquor flowed in abundance. Entertainment was just as grand. The Yellaegba Gba band came from Ziah, the Dahn sisters from Zuatuo, whose soprano voices captivated audiences throughout the entire Lower Nimba, were also there. Others were the Tumba Girls, Morris King, Julius Paye, and his sister, all came to Zuolay, drawing an audience of people never before seen in this picturesque town nestled in Nimba County. From as far away as Zeongein, the intoxicating drumbeat of Shabetto, the legendary drummer from Vahn Town drumbeat, enthralled and mesmerized the singing and dancing crowd. Garretson Biah seems in high spirits, carrying a ceremonial cow tail fleece decorated with cowries shells. A hand-woven gown known as Country Cloth, with Gold embossed threads, adorned his dark, bulky frame.

Dorcas Johnson, an atypical Liberian politician, disliked pomp and pageantry. She was low key for a people who liked their politicians to be loud, flamboyant and generous. She knew how to relate to people, the main reason for her victory in the election. She watched Garretson Biah take all the spotlight, shaking hands and having small talks with the women and youths at the intense frenetic activities going on around her. Dorcas was wearing a simple flowing white gown with matching head tie, and with her only concession to fashion, large red beads around her neck and oversized sunglasses on her face.

The houses in center Zuolay, Bahn's quarter, were arranged in a semi-circle form with the middle reserved for special occasions like this. Oldman Bellker, who worked his farm even on Christmas Day, celebrated among the merrymakers, showing a side of him not seen since he was a boy. As the sunset on the horizon spread its largess into a grateful day, rich hues of red blended with orange, purple and crimsons stretched across the sky far and wide. Dignitaries sitting on the hastily constructed platform, decorated in the national colors of red, white and blue attached to fresh plaited palm fronds and banana trees, rose to offer speeches. The chairman of the Council of Elders, the head of the traditional Zoes, few popular church pastors, the Iman, and the chair lady of the women's organization, one after another, gave their speech. Then Dorcas Johnson took to the podium. Garretson Biah, the esteemed host of the auspicious occasion, had been scheduled to speak last.

"Garretson Biah has shown us what it takes to be a politician," Dorcas Johnson started. "We congratulate a self-made man for his success and extend a warm hand of fellowship as we begin our tenure. We will not hesitate to call upon him whenever we need his words of wisdom while we are on Capitol Hill. I call on our citizens, in and out of District 9, to take the lead of Garretson as we make our district second to none. It is not about who wins or lose, but improving our district." Then she started the call-and-response celebratory chant, "Yor! Yor!"

"Yor," the crowd shouted back.

"What's wrong with District 9," Dorcas Johnson shouted.

"We're alright!"

"Who say so?"

"Everybody!"

"Who's everybody?"

"District 9!"

Dorcas Johnson finished and left the podium. It was time for Garretson to address the crowd.

Ready to address the excited crowd, Garretson raise his clenched fist, and a deafening roar swept across Bahn's quarter. He talked about the strength and joys of unity, before revealing his future plans.

"You all know, I have never sold goods on credit before. But from today, I will change this long-standing policy and lent goods on credit to the poor and needy in our town!"

The crowd reacted like a multi-headed being that shared only one brain. It became dead silent with disbelief. Then when Garretson pumped his fist, it drew thunderous applause from the crowd. They began dancing in jubilation. No one cared why he was being so generous. Every movement in the crowd sent a whirlpool of dust into the air. Garretson had the flair for the dramatic.

"Our Honorable is a gracious person," he continued. "I wish her a long and successful tenure at the Capitol. I, Garretson Biah, henceforth renounce my interest in politics. I propose a toast for our new development agenda for our district."

Garretson uncorked the bottle of gin he was holding and took a sip, feeling the intense burn on his tongue and throat. In that instant, his face tightened as if he had consumed something vinegary. Garretson walked to where a small circular table had been set up with sparkling clear drinking glasses. He poured the drinks into the glasses himself. An employee handed a glass to Honorable Dorcas Johnson, one to the superintendent of Nimba County, and one to Paramount Chief, John Bleatehn. After the last special guest was served, they toasted, clinching their glasses in mid-air.

Garretson kept his hand raised, but with less coordination, and slurred more when he spoke, "Cheeeeeeeers."

He took a step towards the special guests, staggering like an inebriated beggar, invading their space. Then he went down like a sack of cassava in front of the crowd, hitting the ground hard. The gathered crowd wince at the resounding booming sound.

Garretson was out cold. His eyes dilated, and a small mouthful of foam dribbled from his quivering lips. Aides tried helping him to his feet while someone hurried to get a car ready to rush him to the JFD Hospital in Tappeta.

"Check under his fingernails," Paramount Chief, John Bleatehn, said.

The aide picked up Garretson's hand. Not only did his nails showed his hard-working character, but there were also traces of a small amount of brown powder underneath the left index thumbnails.

"It looks like poison," the aide announced.

"So, Garretson brought Honorable Johnson here to poison her," Paramount Chief, John Bleatehn, said.

"It seems so," the aide replied. "We must bury him right away."

And, so the celebration ended that day.

Death is permanent. Dead is forever. And so, Garretson Biah was no more; a victim of his own over-ambition.

## JEAN PIERRE AND KPORMOR

This is a mysterious tale of the falling apart of two very good friends, and the tragic consequences of such falling out when not properly addressed.

# Jean Pierre and Kpormor

In the town of N'Zerekore, located in the mountains along the border of Liberia with Guinea, deep in the tropical forest in the region known as Région forestière, lived two great friends. The deep lush forest surrounding the rural city was nurtured by the high rainfalls from the Guinea highlands of the Nimba mountain. Closer than brothers were Kpormor and Jean Pierre, both physically strong, tall, handsome, and extremely dark in complexion.

Everyone is born with marvelous talents as if we are seeds planted. Kpormor was a master auto mechanic, while Jean Pierre was a gifted carpenter. When Jean Pierre sees a wood, there's a light that dances in his eyes. He was a builder absorbed into the finest of detail of a piece of furniture. His work was always a thing of beauty.

Kpormor, like his friend Jean Pierre, did not go to school. At the age of six, his stepfather sent him to a local mechanic to learn the trade. Boubou, his master, was a thin wiry Muslim who treated Kpormor more like a servant than an apprentice. But Boubou considered the trade of auto mechanic as the prince of trade profession, with whom he had been entrusted to pass sacred knowledge of the trade to the young. Hence, he taught young Kpormor everything he knew about fixing old cars. By the time he was thirteen, Kpormor knew almost everything there was to know about the internal combustion machine. He could diagnose what was wrong with a car by simply listening to the sound of an engine. By age eighteen, Kpormor rebuilt a non-working engine to work as new. He could get any piece of equipment moving, as long as it had an engine.

Whether it was their exceptional talents in their respective trades, their shared passion for hard work, or love for women, or their deep personal magnetism, the two men friendship became legendary.

A typical day for Kpormor and Jean Pierre would be waking up in the morning and having breakfast at either of their places together. Their wives Fanta, Mariamu, and Kema, soon became great friends because their husbands were inseparable. When Kpormor visited Jean Pierre, whether or not her husband was present, Fanta would set the food before Kpormor knowing her husband would receive the same treatment when he went to her friend, Mariamu. Their two youngest sons were both the same age, born less than twenty-four hours apart.

In the ins and outs of human relations and interactions, we do things that deeply offend another person without even realizing what we may have done wrong. But what happened between the two friends one morning in April is so shameful, that the elders forbade the retelling of the story. I can only tell it now because the elders' ban was on oral retelling, and I am writing the story. Technically, I am not violating the elders' ban. Furthermore, like most people, the joys of the forbidden fruit make it even more appealing.

Whatever the reason, no one could be sure. Some people speculated it was a fight over a beautiful Mandingo girl whose smile melted the coldest of hearts. Others said it was a double cross over some money that tore asunder such a beautiful friendship. Kpormor borrowed some money from Jean Pierre to establish his shop, and never paid back even when Kpormor's shop started to prosper. Still, others speculated that it was simply jealousy and envy that drove Jean Pierre to the brink to commit a heinous evil. However, no one could be sure of the underlying reason in the tangle of the relationship. Neither Jean Pierre nor Kpormor spoke to anyone amiss about the other, or complained of any misdeed. What is important is, the end destroyed an entire community.

One morning Jean Pierre dressed in a Senegalese kaftan robe, and a turban on his head, similar to the ones worn by the Tuaregs people of the Sahara, to disguise his appearance. He wore dark sunglasses to conceal his eyes, and Misbaha[1] around his neck, although he was irreligious. He traveled secretly to an obscured destination, southwards toward Liberia. Part of the road from N'Zerekore to Lola was paved. The trip was smooth along this section of road, which ended in Lola. The forest canopy, almost protruding into the town of Lola, gave this area of stability a cool, and pleasant climate.

In Lola, Jean Pierre transferred from a comfortable Toyota bus into an open-top jeep known locally as Kia Motor. The road is the road; when traveling on unpaved dirt roads, one can expect a trail of dust to pester one's nostrils, making one to cough. Jean Pierre was determined in his quest and did not mind the minor inconvenience of dust and the hot sun beating down on him. He was born, and grew up, in the hot humid climate and was used to the low infrastructural development in this part of the world, so he did not mind. More traditional-style houses, roofed with palm thatch, became more prominent in impoverished villages along the road to Beyla, where livestock and people mixed together in perfect harmony, sharing each other diseases and food. Like most Guineans, he spoke several languages fluently; including Kpelle, Mandingo, Soso, and Mano.

Jean Pierre got off the Kia Motor in a small village of three huts and followed a Marabout[2]. The man was a clear head higher than most of the people. He met Jean Pierre's gaze and smiled

---

1 Islamic prayer beads

2 A Muslim holy man believed to have supernatural power.

with his teeth, stained from years of chewing kola nuts. He led Jean Pierre into the forest nearby, whose canopy was so thick that the sunlight could not penetrate its thick foliage. A loud rasping voice, coarse in nature, greeted his presence. Then, unexpectedly, another man, several inches shorter than the Marabout, pushed Jean Pierre into what seems like a blazing fire. Jean Pierre walked through the burning embers to the other side, unharmed. During this transformation, he witnessed flying flamed cowries shells, and a short creature wearing raffia skirts, whose skin looked leathery, go by him. Then, the wind blew through the area with a powerful passion, and a man appeared, frail stature with fiery eyes.

"Son, what can I do for you," the man asked with ghostly voice.

Jean Pierre started to reply but hesitated. The Marabout, too, stood silent. The Mallam[3]  and leathery-skin man encircled them. Jean Pierre sat down, legs crossed. This was no imagination, he was in a trance.

"He should die," Jean Pierre muttered.

Normally, the forest hums with life all around it, but only the shrill chirps of crickets came from the bushes.

"Crawl under that log," the Mallam commanded, the baritone of his voice echoing. He spoke in the local language.

---

3 A honorific title given to Islamic scholars in Africa or medicine man.

Jean Pierre got on his knees. He studied the piece of log held in place by two other scaffold logs supported by strong ropes at opposite ends. As Jean Pierre crawled under the log, he felt its weight become heavy on his back, then pressing him down into the earth. The weight on his shoulders seemed to increase, and he began to struggle. Suddenly, a force lifted his shoulders and he saw a creature whose skin appeared smooth but felt like sand to the touch.

"Come out," the Mallam commanded in a normal human voice.

Jean Pierre crawled out, pulled out the payment and threw the money into a plate.

"My son," the Mallam continued. "The demon of death is who you saw . . . that creature with smooth skin that looked like sand. Once it is released, it cannot come back empty-handed. The only thing that can appease it, or quench its terrible desire for blood, is the blood of your enemy or yourself."

Jean Pierre listened.

"Should I release it," the Mallam asked. "It would be either your blood or that of your enemy. The demon cannot return empty-handed to me."

A man of a pliant mind could have just thrown in the towel and ran from there as fast as his legs could carry him. But Jean Pierre was determined and strong-willed.

"I want him dead," Jean Pierre said, definitely.

"Okay," the Mallam said. "Go, my son. Within twenty-four hours, as soon as you lay eyes on him, he is a dead man. Remember, the demon will not come back empty-handed. If you do not see him by tomorrow evening, you will be a dead man."

Jean Pierre accepted a small animal horn filled with black powder and journeyed back to N'Zerekore.

The presence of refugees from Liberia and Sierra Leone had transformed this sleepy backwater town of N'Zerekore into a blossoming city. It had quickly become the second-largest city in Guinea, surpassing Kankan which used to be the second-largest city. The influx of international aid agencies and humanitarian workers with mouth-watering salaries, by local standards, made this city an affluent town. Duplexes were being built along the road in suburbs like Ossud, and Momou, becoming permanent fixtures of the city. Fleets of Toyota Land Cruisers now competed with badly repaired Japanese taxicabs and French Peugeot cars for space in the narrow streets.

Jean Pierre got out of the Land Cruiser with spring in his steps when he arrived back in his city. Finally, he had avenged in the most extreme way possible. The thought brought him pleasure, like taking a beautiful woman on a first date. He greeted his wife heartily at the door of the family homestead. A song played in his heart, he had planned it well. No one knew about his trip to the Marabout. His secret was safe, the animal horn with black congealed powder, tucked away deep in his trouser pockets.

Jean Pierre could not wait for the day to break. A man with an important mission, he wanted to see Kpormor and see him fast. As the saying goes in North-eastern Liberia; 'The thing a man stayed in the town for and did not go to his farm, is something that has to be done with urgency.'

Fanta, his wife, being a traditional married woman, woke up early to prepare her husband breakfast, boiled ripe plantain dipped in red oil gravy sauce.

Jean Pierre hurriedly brushed his teeth, washed his face, and soon after, headed for the door.

"Fanta," he said, "I will be back soon."

"At least, eat something small," Fanta urged.

"I'll be back soon," he said. "I am going to get Kpormor so we can enjoy this delicious breakfast together. It looks too good to eat it alone. I must share it with him."

It was the usual thing for these friends to eat together. In fact, they often did. But Fanta would have loved for her husband to eat some of her food before leaving the house. Before she could utter another word, Jean Pierre was already out the door, whistling.

Kpormor lived in Ossud, a small community at the other side of the swamp from the UN's office. It was one of those compounds where several families lived together in simple apartments of one to two bedrooms, with the entrance doors facing the front or common area. Although there was a road wide enough for a car to travel to where Kpormor lived, Jean Pierre took the shorter footpath through the swamp. Morning market-ers were already on their way to the market with their wares on their heads, or in wheelbarrows.

Jean Pierre knocked on Kpormor's door.

There was no element of surprise when Mariamu, Kpormor's wife, opened the door. She smiled. Mariamu was a mixture of Fulani, Mandingo, and Kpelle, which showed in her elegant features.

"Kpormor is not here," she informed Jean Pierre. "I thought he came to your place to have breakfast with you. Maybe you both were heading in opposite directions or may have used different routes. I cooked some eddoes and yams .. . also some rice porridge. Would you like to have some?"

"I won't keep Kpormor waiting," Jean Pierre said. "I will leave now. Your sister, Fanta, cooked some delicious ripe plantain breakfast. We will eat there, and then come here and eat your breakfast."

"Alright," Mariamu agreed. "Say good morning to my sister, Fanta."

The women were not biological siblings, they had become close friends, like sisters, in the true sense of the word, like their husbands were as close as brothers.

Jean Pierre hurried away. He needed to see Kpormor fast. He was positive that Kpormor would be sitting by now, chatting with Fanta. Once he sees Kpormor, he would watch mournfully as his friend pass away, while being inwardly gleeful. No one was going to suspect a thing.

"Where is Kpormor," Fanta asked, as soon as Jean Pierre entered the yard.

Jean Pierre frowned.

"You said the both of you were coming back here," Fanta reminded him. "Now the food I have cooked is getting cold while you wander."

"Kpormor is not here yet," Jean Pierre asked, ignoring his wife's quarrel.

"Obviously not," Fanta replied, "as you can see."

"Mariamu said he left the house early without a bag or anything, for that matter. She thought he was headed here for us to have breakfast. He should be here soon," he said. "I took the short-cut back."

Jean Pierre's words were meant more as a re-assurance to himself.

An hour later when Kpormor had not arrived, Jean Pierre seemed a little agitated. He could not waste precious time waiting around the house. It was a workday, and people were waiting for him at the shop. He could not call Kpormor to see where he was either. This was before easy access to mobile phone. Those days when you wanted to know where a person was, you had to go looking for them. You drove or walked to their house, hoping they'd be home. Not to make his wife more irritated, Jean Pierre hurriedly ate his breakfast, although it tasted like nothing. He re-membered a bed he had to deliver to a rich cus-tomer and hurried to his shop.

At work, Jean Pierre became easily irritated. His apprentices sensed something was wrong.

He delivered their instructions with less emotion than usual. By mid-morning Jean Pierre remembered one of their favorite hangout places. He and Kpormor often met at a bar on the outskirts of the rural city to drink palm wine while they waited for others to join. Even though it was still morning, the place was crowded mostly with loafers and guys who were simply too friendly with the bottle. Alcohol was usually easy to get, even when one did not have money to buy. Patrons were generous in buying and sharing their drinks. He wanted to go back to Kpormor's place for the second time this morning but thought that would raise suspicion. Jean Pierre scanned the group of men sitting and drinking while discussing local politics.

"Guys, have any of you seen Kpormor," he asked when he approached the group.

An old acquaintance named Kollie laughed.

"My brother," Kollie said, "this is not a parking station to come asking for someone. Here, have a glass of palm wine," he offered. "The taste is refreshing."

"Kollie, I did not come to drink your leftover," Jean Pierre replied. "I can buy my own. I simply asked if any of you have seen my friend, Kpormor, this morning."

Kollie turned to the man standing by him and asked, "Have you seen Kpormor?"

The man replied, "No."

Each man asked the man standing next to him if any had seen Kpormor that morning. The last man said, "Sorry, Jean Pierre, no one has seen Kpormor since yesterday."

Being scared is normal, but this was different. Jean Pierre's heart began pounding in his chest. What was happening? He hailed a motorbike taxi to take him to Kpormor's place of work. They could have lunch. They always had lunch together unless one of them was out of town. Kpormor had not mentioned to him about leaving N'Zerekore for business or any other reason. Kpormor had to be in town.

Today the sunshine seemed brighter, its heat radiating outwards into the bright day. Vehicles of all kinds, laden with goods, traveled back and forth, some dodging potholes when it could. Jean Pierre did not bother haggling with the motorbike driver for the price. He instructed the driver to take him to Kpormor's workplace.

Kpormor was not at the shop. This was getting serious. Kpormor had to die for his transgression. The price to pay if that did not happen was too terrible for Jean Pierre to contemplate. Jean Pierre took another motorbike taxi to his friend's house. He saw the shock register on Mariamu's face when he asked about her husband again.

"No, Jean Pierre," Mariamu said. "Kpormor has not been here since this morning."

"Did he go out of town?"

"He did not say he was going out of town."

"Are you sure?"

"He did not have a bag with him when he was leaving. Kema and I should be the one asking you

for our husband since you both know each other's whereabouts."

"I've been to his shop . . . he was not there,"
Jean Pierre said. "He did not come to my house
for breakfast, or by my shop. I've even checked
our hang out spots . . . no one has seen him. No
one has a clue where Kpormor is."

"I hope Kpormor has not met a new woman,"
Mariamu said, frowning. "You two are trying to
fool us, pretending that you don't know where he
is."

"I'm not pretending, Mariamu."

"Did you check your favorite palm wine
station?"

Jean Pierre nodded.

Mariamu furrowed her brow.

"Jean Pierre, don't come back here without
my husband," Mariamu said. "Either bring him
home or bring back concrete information of his
whereabouts. This is strange," she shook her
head.

"Yes, it is quite strange," Jean Pierre agreed.

He was glad Kema, the feisty wife, was not at
home.

Mariamu's puzzled expression and abrupt respond made Jean Pierre uneasy. There was a look
of genuine concerns on the man's wife's face.
Then again, he had to find Kpormor.

The time came during the day when palm
wine tappers would bring fresh wine from the
farms in large white jerry cans. The men of this
town were notorious winebibbers. Many a dis-

pute was settled in the intoxicating ambiance of the palm wine tree.

Surely, Kpormor could be at their favorite hangout place at sunset, he thought. Jean Pierre stopped by Kpormor's shop on his way to the palm wine station. He wasn't there.

Most palm wine sellers are women while the majority of their customers are men of all ages. Rows of low thatch-roofed houses lined the road to the palm wine station. All men are treated equally here, regardless of social status. Jean Pierre changed tack. Instead of pacing and asking for Kpormor like a police interrogatory, he joined the first group of men he encountered drinking palm wine in one of those huts. Jean Pierre down a big cup of wine, enjoying the mild alcoholic brew. He licked the foam of the drink off his mustache. The talk in the hut he was in turned to politics, about the upcoming municipal election which often inflamed ethnic tensions among the Kpelle and Mandingo ethnic groups. The people usually got along well until politicians bereft of ideas and platforms, exploiting these divisions for political purposes.

Jean Pierre did not care for political talk. He had more pressing personal concerns. He scanned the faces but did not see his friend, Kpormor. After spending what he considered sufficient time in the hut, Jean Pierre walked to the next hut. There was nothing suspicious about what he was doing now since men often drifted from one palm wine hut to the other. He did that for a while, moving from one palm wine hut to another, keeping an eagle eye for Kpormor.

What the hell was happening? How come Kpormor had suddenly vanished? Kpormor did not inform him about leaving town, he would have been the first person to know. Jean Pierre kept the furious grudge against his friend under tight wraps and had not shown by word, or action, anything akin to that. Neither would Kpormor leave town without a word to his wives, or the boys working in his shop. Jean Pierre had not revealed his visit to the Marabout or to anyone, not even his wife. There was no way Kpormor could fathom his plans. Jean Pierre broke his silence in the fifth hut and asked for Kpormor.

"My friend, why do you keep looking for Kpormor like a man searching for his wife?" One man asked. "Go to the man's house and ask his wives . . . let people drink in peace."

Jean Pierre remembered the man was at the palm wine station this morning. He spat in disgust, though he would rather slap the annoying man in the face to teach him a lesson about controlling his flippant tongue. On second thought, he did not do so because he did not want to draw attention to himself. The powdered horn in his trousers pocket dug deeper into his skin. He was at wit's end, and desperation was beginning to set in. His brain was on fire and he could not remember where else to search for Kpormor. The sunset reminded him of that. He staggered toward another palm wine shop.

"My people, have any of you seen Kpormor," Jean Pierre yelled, tears now filling his eyes.

Everyone momentarily paused, their drinks reaching halfway to their mouths, many shaking their heads, 'No'.

"Kpormor has not been here today," one woman said. "We should be asking you. You two are like the teeth and tongue."

This brought laughter.

Jean Pierre was now a man on fire, a crazy man; running to his house on motorbike taxis, then rushing back to Kpormor's house. Also, his hasten inquiries bringing puzzled stares and doubt to the familiar faces. Now his life seemed a misty blur.

Jean Pierre soon became a broken man. Tears ran down his face. He wondered if he would see his wife and children again. Would he be able to continue his work at his beloved workshop? A Marabout could sometimes lie, he thought. Impostors took your money, and that was it. If something happens by chance, in the direction one wishes, they would claim that as evidence of their prowess. And, if what they predicted failed, they would always find a way to blame those who consulted them in the first place, exonerating themselves. Jean Pierre wished this was true in this case. A few hours ago he was desperate for the medicine man's evil charms to work. Now that he could not find Kpormor, he prayed the charm fail.

Twenty-four hours had passed when Jean Pierre got home. He went straight to his room and shut the door. The room filled with smoke, and in it, the leathery creature appeared. Jean Pierre dare ask for pity because mercy to this creature meant death. He was tasked with taking a departing soul and not going back empty-handed. The angel of death was here, and Jean Pierre was about to die. And so as his body made ready to die, he thought of his life. Then, he was gone.

A few hours later, Jean Pierre's family discovered his lifeless body. Their crying came loud and endless. Neighbors rushed in from far and wide to console his wives. In line with Muslim traditions, arrangements were being made for burial as soon as possible.

The next morning, Kpormor appeared at his house only to find his wives confused and in tears. They did not know how to break the news about his friend.

"I know what happened," Kpormor told them before anyone could break the news. "This is something Jean Pierre brought on himself," he said.

"What are you saying," Mariamu said, drying her eyes.

Kpormor than calmly proceeded to tell his wife how his dear friend and brother, Jean Pierre, had taken his life to a Marabout, not knowing the Marabout's chief assistant was his mother's younger brother. His young uncle had hastened to warn him, suggesting that he leave town immediately. To go away as far as possible, he had gone to Kissidougou, gotten a hotel and locked himself away. No one was to know until after twenty-four hours.

How a remarkable story ended in tragedy has been forbidden to be told by the elders. This story I heard in hushed whispers one night when my parents thought I'd been sleeping. I listened well and copied the story to my memory. I wanted to tell the story to another person because no one has been able to fathom what Kpormor did to Jean Pierre that irked him to take such desperate measures. Mindful of the elders' interdiction, this story needed to be told. I am western educated, but I am emotionally bound by the edits of my elders. The good thing is, I am not telling this story to another person, I'm writing it; thus, I am free from violating the taboo placed on telling this story in an oral manner as per our tradition.

## Old But Not Cold

---

In the settlement along the fertile banks of the St. Paul River, *Old But Not Cold* is an unconventional love story between an alcoholic old man whose life had dealt cruel blows of experiments and surprises, and a jilted young woman whose unfaithful boyfriend constantly breaks her heart. Respect existence, or expect resistance; the coming together of two seemingly different people shows love can strike in the least expected way to the least expected people.

# Old But Not Cold

The old man sipped the strong gin known as Cecelia Johnson by the settlers who farm alongside the fertile banks of the St. Paul River. The rich soil was better suited for the most demanding crop, sugarcane. However, the sweet juice from the thick stalk of the cane plant was not used to make sugar, or molasses, like in other parts of the world, but to make gin. The sugary juice is squeezed out of the plant and stored at the right temperature, then heated, allowed to cool by passing through a drum filled with water, converting the steam into the liquid to produce the potent gin called, cane juice. The liquor is usually sold in dingy bars across the settlements[1] and in Monrovia. One did not need to have a liquor license to sell

---

1 Small communities formed along the St. Paul River during the establishment of Liberia, including Caldwell, Clay Ashland, Arthington, Crozierville, Bensonville, etc.

this bootleg liquor. Anyone wanting to sell this gin only needed a few tables, chairs, and glasses, preferably plastic cups, and a handwritten sign; they would be in business.

Oldman Adolphus Deshield brought the liquid bottle to his weather-cracked lips and let the clear fluid sit in his mouth a while before swallowing. He closed his eyes, dwelling on the flavor. It was good, just what he needed. Cane juice turns down the volume on one's thoughts. It steals away reality in favor of a temporary world of calmness and bliss.

Adolphus did not mind the boisterous chatter of a group of unemployed young men noisily discussing politics about the misrule of President Tubman, although the man had been dead long before most of them were born. These young men took comfort in blaming past leaders as a cure for the social and economic problems of Liberia instead of offering solutions. There were a couple of young women among them. As the night wore on, the crowd in the shabby shop decreased.

Oldman Adolphus had seen better days. A Howard University graduate in the 1960s, he'd returned from America to the position of Assistant Minister at the Ministry of Information, in charge of research. A wealthy family of landowners, the Deshields owned valuable pieces of real estate in central Monrovia, Sinkor, along the Robertsfield highway, and even in Bentol and Arthington. The Liberian government was tenant to the Deshields, leasing two buildings that housed the Ministry of Youth and Sports, and the Ministry of Education. Admiring the lifestyle of the southern plantations in the United States, Adolphus bought land in Crozierville, along the White Plains corridor, hoping one day to plant rubber, cocoa, sugarcane and other cash crops in the rich soil.

Like many Liberian elites, he made the same mistake by sending his children, still very young, to the West to study. These youngsters quickly adapted the lifestyle of the West and did not return to the homeland. His oldest daughter, Mildred, lived and worked as an RN in Minneapolis, Minnesota. Adolphus Jr., his oldest son, made Washington DC his home, serving that community as a medical doctor. And his youngest son, Theodore, having resisted medicine, worked as a journalist in London. The one blight on this family who had been expected to be a model of virtues among his children was Danielle Anne, who had succumbed to drugs, one of the vilest temptations to young people. She had become a drug addict lost in New York City.

The poorly lit bar was almost empty now. A young woman sitting alone on the bar stool struggled to swallow her gin from the glass. The fiery liquid burned her mouth and seemed difficult to swallow, as would be for someone who was not used to it. Her black braids flowed all the way down to her back. It gave contrast to her face, a perfect blend of browns from her skin to her dress. The woman looked twenty-something.

"To swallow the gin, you just gulp it down," Adolphus suggested. "Then, it won't burn so much."

Startled, she turned and looked at the old man staring at her. She couldn't decide whether to tell the old hag to mind his own business or remain quiet. Adolphus kept staring. Even in the dimly lit shabby room, he could tell she had been crying.

"What do you care," she finally said. "You men are all dogs."

Adolphus kept staring without saying a word.

"Why do men act like that," she continued. "A woman meets a man, falls in love with him and gives him everything . . . her life, her heart, her mind, and even her body . . . and still, that isn't enough for him."

She gulped down the fiery liquid and furrowed her brow. Tears filled her eyes like it would anyone who is not used to drinking strong alcohol.

"I gave Tamba my heart . . . guess what he did," the woman continued, rhetorically. "I caught him sleeping with my best friend. The idiot had the nerve to tell me he could explain such action. Explain what? That he was a cheating, conniving man who destroyed my friendship. And, as for Weade, she will feel pepper. . . I'm going to deal with her later."

The words were tumbling out of her mouth and she was sobbing. Adolphus wanted to go and hold her to comfort her. But how could the sniveling old man with alcohol on his breath do that, without being accused of taking advantage of a distraught young woman?

"My name is, Adolphus," the old man introduced himself. He sat on the empty stool next to the woman. "When people are facing hard situations, they usually turn to God, drugs, or alcohol. Sometimes, combining one or two, or all three. Your boyfriend must be a pig to cheat on you with your best friend."

The woman forced a smile, showing dimples in both cheeks.

"A pig is better than Tamba," she replied, and launched another attack against her boyfriend, or ex-boyfriend.

Adolphus wondered which was which; a boyfrend or an ex-boyfriend. He listened to her rant, which sometimes descended into an incoherent mumble. There was something in that rant, something like pain behind it. He watched the woman's eyes. The anger was nothing but a shield for her pain, perhaps scared for loneliness. He took a big sip of his gin.

As soon as the plastic cup left his lips, Adolphus said, "Young women today would rather go out with men their own age." He held on to his cup and waited for the woman to say something. When she didn't, he said, "But, these young men . . . at least most of them, are too busy experimenting and exchanging women. That's because they have not learned to appreciate the finer things in life, like the company of a beautiful, intelligent, young woman."

The woman barked out a laugh and said, "What would a young woman do with an old man who has lived his life? Wouldn't she be wasting her young life being with an old goat?"

Adolphus let out a chuckle.

"By the way, my name is, Bernadette," the woman introduced herself. "But, I'd rather be single, than consider being with an old man."

This time, Adolphus let out a scornful laugh.

"Bernadette," he said, "being old does not mean a man is cold. An old man can still do what he'd done before."

"Look," the shop owner interrupted. "It's almost midnight, Adolphus, I have to close now." Then she turned to look at Bernadette. "Fine girl, I'm about to close. Don't mind this old man . . . he likes to talk. If you mind him, you would stay here until day breaks . . . and he would still be talking."

Ma Kebbeh, the shop owner, was a middle-aged, thin woman. Life is mostly downhill from twenty, and the slop only gets steeper from forty. Some people become kinder, wiser, or truer to the inner person they want to be. Guessing for a woman, as the wrinkles deepen over her face, she hopes the positive effect of her life affects the lives of others.

"It's late," Ma Kebbeh said, "I need to close up and go to bed."

"Didn't you open this place for us to enjoy ourselves while you make a profit?" Adolphus said. "We're still drinking, and you're talking about closing."

"I have a husband who's waiting for me," Ma Kebbeh replied. "Your wife left you for the bright lights of New York, so you come here to wallow in the mud and drink my cheap liquor."

Adolphus furrowed his brow.

He turned to Bernadette and asked, "Where do you live, young lady?"

"And what has that got to do with you, old man," she replied.

"Well, I thought you might need a lift to Crozierville, which is just across the way."

"Thanks, but no thanks," Bernadette replied. "I can take care of myself."

Bernadette cleared her throat as she tried standing, just to fall back down on the stool in an unbalanced attempt to walk. Although Adolphus had been drinking, the old man was not drunk. He managed to help Bernadette to her feet and assisted her to his beat-up Ford pickup parked next to the building.

Adolphus used the familiar back roads north of the capital, connecting the settlements to Monrovia. He followed her directions to a large building anchored on concrete pillars that ran into the ground, with a large veranda typical of early 20th Century architecture Pioneer houses. She got out of the car and thanked him. Adolphus waited until she had safely entered her home before driving away.

Oldman Adolphus thought about the young woman in the days that followed, and hoped to see her again. The thing is, he could not remember where he had dropped her off that night. He frequented Ma Kebbeh's bar the following weeks, but she was never there. He wondered if she had made up with her cheating boyfriend. What he should be thinking about was his wrinkled face, arthritic joints and the sore on his left foot, which could probably be cancerous.

Bernadette McCritty woke up the following morning with a stubborn headache that had not gone away even after taking two aspirins. She ran herself a hot bath, removed her clothes, and slid down into the tub of hot water, letting it block out the sound around her. The hot water made her feel better. Her mind suddenly drifted from Tamba to the old man who had taken her home last night. Then it went back to Tamba. She'd loved him wholeheartedly, especially his sophisticated manners and infectious smile which brought sunshine into her life. She couldn't understand the betrayal. Why had he betrayed her with Lucille Padmore, of all people, her best friend?

How quickly love was turning into hate. If she was not careful, the negative emotion would swallow her or pour acid into her soul. The pain had constricted her throat, making it difficult for her to breathe at times. She'd even felt a tight lump in her throat. Food tasted like sand in her mouth. But humans, however, have an incredible ability to bounce back from adversity. A new life would mean, when she recovers, she would never have anything to do with a man again . . . any man.

Bensonville[2] was a short distance from Bernadette's home in Crozierville. Its market day fell on Tuesday, and people from neighboring towns

---

2 Capital of Montserrado County

and villages, as far away as Kakata, Monrovia, and Firestone, congregated to this colorful outdoor market. A lot went on, not just buying and selling, but also to socialize and share the latest geez[3] from the settlements and suburbs. Bernadette dressed in simple jeans skirt, white blouse, and light brown sandals, and headed to the market. She vowed never to visit Ma Kebbeh bar again.

A year went by. Adolphus went to the bar often, hoping to see the young woman again, but was not lucky. There's always hope in the future. In that future developed an unlikely match between a conservative, well-educated, old man whose once-promising life had gone down because of marital deceits, bitterness and alcohol, and a vivacious young woman whose heart was firmly set on the future although she was nursing a broken heart. Oldman Adolphus Deshield transported marketers with their wares to the market for a small fee. It was then that on one of these trips he noticed a beautiful young woman who had greeted him with a bright smile. Neither had remembered anything about the night they first met at Ma Kabbeh's bar, until months later.

It is when you are in need of hope when your heart has broken into a million pieces, that your soul reaches out to make the bond of real friendship. Importantly, that friendship must have a foundation of trust. Each friend must come with a fresh mind, not thinking of a future, nor the past. That's when the good stuff begins.

---

3 Gossips

Helping each other was a blessing, as it was the way they loved one another and with gratitude. Bernadette took interest in the old man's stories when she went to give his house a good clean, or make a nice home-cooked meal. Each time she did that for her friend, he gifted her with a good book, and hope they would have something to discuss when she comes back. Adolphus told her about life in Monrovia during the 1960s and '70s, boasting of the heydays when Monrovia had American banks like Chase Manhattan, and Citibank, as well as big Chevy cars. He spoke fondly of student life at Howard, and his return to a government job working for the flamboyant President Tubman.

Bernadette got teased relentlessly by her friends for spending so much time with an old man. But she continued servicing her friend's needs, like cleaning his house, cooking his food, and nursing the sore on his leg. Old Adolphus gifted her with expensive things and entertained her with more stories of his youthful years. The friendship blossomed, and Bernadette laughed more often. She stopped listening to Tamba Johnny's phony apologies and finally asked him to leave.

Tamba Johnny responded with, "Are you leaving me because of a crazy old man with a rotten leg?"

Bernadette told him she wasn't leaving him for anyone. It was because of his disrespect toward her when she had done him no wrong.

Tamba Johnny did not leave quietly, to say the least, but the relationship was over.

Adolphus hardly visited the bar.

Many had walked Adolphus' life before, and share the scars that mark their body, mind, and spirit. Thankfully, what he had suffered at his own hand, and those of others, had brought forth new opportunities for change.

One evening as they kept company, Adolphus turned to his friend and said, "What do you see in a troublesome old man like me?"

Bernadette laughed.

"Nothing," she said and began rubbing Adolphus' thin gray hair. "However, underneath this old body lies a beautiful heart. Do you know . . . my parents were quite old when they had me. I'm used to being around old people, but, this old man," she touched his arm, "touch me in a way and I don't know if I like that."

"I cannot help it, Bernadette," Adolphus said.

Bernadette smiled.

"I've made many mistakes in my life," Adolphus said, "and I want an opportunity to fix things."

"Mistakes?"

"I worked hard to acquire properties for my children here in Liberia, but I sent them to America when they were too young. They have no interest in things here because they'd rather live in America. I became a cripple because of my accident. It wasn't my fault, but it changed my life. Then my wife abandoned me, sold most of my properties and took off with a much younger man. Now all she does is, wait to see if I have any more money to take. I am too old, and too drunk, to stop her. Having met you, I've been thinking about divorcing her . . . if you would agree to marry me."

"Marry you," Bernadette sighed. "What would people say?"

"That I am sucking your young blood," Adolphus joked.

Bernadette chuckled.

"What woman would refuse a marriage proposer from the esteemed Adolphus Deshield," she said.

"Not you, I hope."

"The truth is, I've fallen in love with you," Bernadette confessed. "It would be a pleasure to be your wife. But, would I have to tote you to the altar because you're too drunk to walk?"

"I hardly drink these days," he said. "You have changed my life. I have more reason to be sober. Besides," he kissed the back of her hand, "I want to have better memories before I died."

"This is no time to talk about death, Adolphus," Bernadette said and kissed his cheek. "We are talking about getting married. We should be talking about our future."

In the main time . . . .

It's easy for people to manipulate the truth, regardless, news travels fast. Adolphus' wife, Weade, heard with growing alarm about the liaison between her estranged husband and a young woman. As long as Adolphus was drunk, it suited her purpose. She could scam him out of all his money. And finally, when he drank himself to death, she would be right there, besides their children, to benefit from his earnings. Weade consulted with her lawyer and they hastily drew up a will, Adolphus making his wife, Weade, the principal beneficiary of his inheritance.

Weade boarded the earliest flight from JFK Airport to Liberia. She felt the heat-reflecting tropical climate as they came out of the plane. The people moved with ease from the plane to the arrivals area where a mixture of bored and excited people waited for friends and relatives. Weade went from the terminal building and into a taxi, wasting no time driving to the old house.

As soon as she got there, she cooked Adolphus his favorite food, fufu and pepper soup, lauding it with crawfish. Like always, Weade served the food with plenty of liquor. Adolphus, though surprised by Weade's visit, was prepared. He had already filed for divorce and paid Bernadette's dowry. To Weade's advantage, Bernadette had gone to care for a sick aunt across St. Paul's bridge, a little way from the settlement. Not only did he refuse her food and liquor, but Weade could not talk him into signing the will she'd drawn up with her lawyer in New York. Not even the anger in her eyes made him do something he did not want to do, but it took a toll on the old man. She had tried grabbing him by his neck, threatening to choke him. Adolphus refused to do what Weade wanted him to do. As quickly as she had come, Weade left Liberia on the first available flight to America.

Bernadette returned to a frightened old man, his neck swollen and with visible fingerprints. The roughing up had taken Adolphus' voice. He could not speak. Bernadette quickly hired a taxi and transported him to St. Joseph's Hospital. There was not much the doctor could do for Adolphus. However, more determined than ever, the old man requested a pen and paper to write is words. He ripped the paper in two, scribbled something on one piece, and shove it in Bernadette's hand. She looked at the piece of paper and read to herself what he had written: *Do not open the content of the first letter I gave you until after my death.*

She touched his arm softly.

"You are not going to die, Adolphus," she sobbed. "Please, don't leave me."

Adolphus closed his eyes, his limbs staying still. The sound of Bernadette's crying grew fainter, and then he was no more.

The coffin was expertly crafted not to bring comfort to the dearly departed, but to soothe the living. Adolphus Deshield laid in the bronze casket dressed in the finest suit money could buy. Along with Weade, Adolphus' children had returned to bury their father, all except Danielle Ann, who remained in New York looking for her next high. Weade, who wasn't crying, forced tears to drip down her face from eyes sporting oversized black sunglasses. She was a perfect shining example of a grieving widow, experiencing the deep sadness of the death of a beloved husband. Officials of government and other statesmen attending the funeral consoled the grieving widow. A long procession of cars accompanied the body from the Zion Grove Baptist Church to the cemetery. Throughout the ceremonies, Bernadette mourned alone.

Soon everyone returned to their former lives.

Bernadette missed the eccentric old man. Her friends continued to laugh at her for wasting her time with a senile old man.

"His wife and children took everything, and left you with nothing," they joked.

She had forgotten all about Adolphus letter until one day her friend, Latoyo, came for a visit.

"Bernadette, you are young," she said. "Forget about the old man who is in the grave. He is useless now. Get on with your life."

"I made him happy," Bernadette replied. "He was not a useless man."

"He wasn't?" Latoyo asked.

"Regardless of what people were saying, we were going to get married."

"But you didn't. You are left with nothing now. His wife got everything."

"He gave me something before he died."

"He did," Latoyo said incredulously. "What did he give you?"

"A letter."

Bernadette ran to her room to fetch the letter, then ran back to her friend with the letter in hand.

"This letter," she show Latoyo the crumbled piece of paper, and sat down.

Bernadette opened the letter, looked at it, and frowned.

"What is it?" Latoyo asked.

"It's written in code," Bernadette said. "I don't understand it."

Latoyo took the letter and inspected it. The only thing legible was the name of a lawyer, Ophelia Richards.

"Maybe this, Ophelia Richards, would understand it," Latoyo suggested.

"Maybe," Bernadette said. "We should go see her."

The women took a taxi to Ophelia Richards' office.

The lawyer studied the letter for a while. Then, her face lit up and she looked at Bernadette.

"That old rascal," she said, laughing. You're right . . . the letter is written in code. But, I've figured it out."

Bernadette smiled.

"To make sense of it, each word meant to communicate the message is actually after the third letter. See," she pointed it out to Bernadette.

"What do you mean," Bernadette asked.

"You are a rich woman, Miss McCritty," the lawyer said. "Adolphus Deshield left you 100 acres of prime farmland in Kakata, on the Monrovia-Kakata highway. He also left you two houses, one in Buchanan, and a five-bedroom house in Jacob Town. There is a bank account containing thirty thousand US dollars, which you are the sole beneficiary, at Access Bank. The check is written to you, and it's kept in a safe behind the wall where the bed is."

The loss of words said more. Words left Bernadette and her friend, Latoyo, as well. Neither could will their lips to move.

"I don't know what to say," Bernadette said. "Is it a joke, or what?"

"It's not a joke," the lawyer said. She handed Bernadette what looked like a piece of document. "Sign here. You could retain me as your lawyer, or get someone else."

Bernadette took her time to read the document. She looked at Latoyo when she was finished.

"Is it true?" Latoyo asked.

"Yes, it is true," Bernadette said, nodding her head.

"I would be glad to be your lawyer," Ophelia Richards offered. "I'm familiar with Adolphus Deshield's estate. He left the family house to his wife, Weade, as well as some investment bonds, and cash to his grandchildren, payable when they reach the ages of twenty-one."

Bernadette's hands trembled as she held the pen carefully in her right hand. She remembered the smile on Adolphus' face when he took his last breath. She considered his words on the first night they met at the bar, "I am old, but not cold." She smiled. With her signature, everything the document says is hers. She felt Adolphus's warmth inside as she signed her signature on the paper.

In that simple act, Bernadette Yiley McCritty became a wealthy young woman. All because of one fateful night when she met an eccentric old man whom she grew to love, and who loved her even in his grave, and would be taking care of her for the rest of her life.

## Sea Breeze

Set in postwar Liberia, a young man succumbed to the temptations of armed robbery, and takes along the young woman who loved his despicable characters, irrespective of being in harm's way.

# Sea Breeze

Now that they were separated, would she see him again?

The pain in her left leg was almost unbearable. Facing a court order and lying in pain on the small hospital bed, her thoughts were on him. Her left hand was handcuffed to the bed while medicines poured into the veins in her right hand from a tube, giving her a chance to live. Everything and everyone appeared like a white maze. She continued to mumble a name, "Junior . . . Junior . . . ." Even in excruciating pain, the young woman was attractive; sporting an oval face, curly hair, straight nose, full lips, and a chocolate complexion. Her regular breathing confirmed her life was no longer in danger.

In the densely populated suburb of Pipeline, many persons could not hide their disgust with the girl. Some were openly rejoicing that Junior, whom she was crying for, was in critical condition. Many hoped he would die and go to meet his Creator.

Every night the poor people living on Duport Road in Paynesville, cringed in their homes, being terrorized by ruthless gangs of men. In fact, they were mere boys who held nothing sacred and did not care whether it was an old grandmother, or a crying toddler they struck; prowling, ransacking, looting, and at times raping, their helpless victims. A quick getaway was their hallmark. Strong bodied young men cowered in fear when Junior struck. Even having steel doors did not keep the people safe. Junior and his gang took them down when he wanted to. The Police did not deter him either, especially when most officers only cared about the five dollars bribes they extorted from taxi drivers.

Even in her confused mind, Lovely, the girl under Police guard, remembered when she first saw Junior; a tall, dashing fellow. Junior's hand glittered with gold rings and an expensive watch. His face lit up when their eyes met, and he smiled. The young man was a suave, elegant, fellow, offering free liquor and goat soup to everyone in the barroom. The small dingy bar served many regular customers, including well-to-do men with their escorts of underage girls dressed in classic high fashion. There was a little bit more of everything, from too much lipsticks to too much jewelry, and too much exposed bare flesh. The owner of the barroom, Ma Musu, was a large boisterous woman who had come to the city many years ago as a child from the north. All of her customers looked forward to this tasty pepper soup made with goat meat.

Lovely wasted no time ditching the pot-bellied fifty-year-old former Minister from the Gyude Bryant administration. When Junior smiled and beckoned her, she hurriedly joined him on the dance floor to the beat of 2-Face's African Queen. Everyone inside the entertainment spot held their breath, struck by the beauty of the young couple swaying their bodies in a perfect rhythmic style.

Not far from there, residents propped their windows and doors with anything they could find; pans, dishes, shovels, and old chairs. Their efforts were gear to alerting them when the men who inflicted terror at night intruded upon their homes. But whether one was awake or asleep, when the armed gang struck, it made no difference.

"How beautiful you are," Junior said when the music stopped. "What's your name?"

"Lovely," she replied, leaning toward him.

"I'm Rodney, but my friends call me, Junior. Call me Junior, you are now my friend."

He had ignored the thing while they were dancing, but Junior's mobile phone started ringing again, nonstop. He put his hand in his pocket, pulled out something and scribbled on it. Then, he took Lovely's hand, placed the piece of paper in it, and hurried away. Lovely open her hand, gawking at the one hundred US dollar bill with his phone number on it.

In the main time at the home of a wealthy businessman, one Mr. Danny Lomar, his wife, holding on to their baby, sat screaming in terror. Some of their belongings; smartphones, money, clothes, and jewelry had been piled into bags by some armed robbers. Mr. Lomar sat covering his face, trying to stop the blood pouring from a gash in his forehead. He had sustained his injuries because of the despicable activities of the four armed men wearing hoods and brandishing their AK-47 assault rifles in his face. Distrustful of local banks, Mr. Lomar had kept his valuables at home in a safe. He sat helpless, fuming as he watched his life savings being confiscated by the armed gang. The fact that they had treated his wife in a callous manner while his children cried in terror.

The following morning Lovely got a call from Junior, asking her to meet him at a remote farm resort not far from Monrovia. You can only get to know about a person over time. The two met several times with mutual attraction, thus the love affair began. Lovely willingly did everything, and anything, to please Junior, whose dashing ways seemed appealing to her. One minute he was Prince Charming, and the next minute he was a raging mad man. School, church, and things good girls did slipped further down her list of priorities. Since their meeting, all Lovely wanted was a fast life, good food, fine jewelry, expensive liquor, and the varied nightlife Junior offered.

The first time Lovely introduced Junior to her mother, the woman took one look at him and said, "My daughter, if you follow this boy, he will bring you nothing but trouble."

Blinded by love, Lovely did not care for her mother's warning. Then one day Junior told her what she already suspected.

"Lovely, I think by now you know who I am, right?"

"You are the best man in the whole world," Lovely replied.

While Lovely's spirit reeked with the infectious enthusiasm of one in love, junior's showed signs of a possessive man demanding the attention of a woman he claims to love.

"I wasn't talking about that," Junior said. "I was referring to how I make a living."

"You mean the cars and jewelry you have?"

"People think I'm a dangerous man," Junior said. "What do you think?"

"I know," Lovely replied, almost smiling. "But, I love you."

"Just me, right," he said, suddenly grabbing her by the neck, his hands tightening around her throat.

Lovely struggled for breath.

"Answer me so I can remove my hand," Junior demanded.

She nodded.

Junior removed his hand, smiling with satisfaction. "I love you so much," he said. "I don't want anyone else to even look at you."

Lovely touched his hand.

"It's only you that I love," she said and began stroking it.

"Good . . . good," he said and kissed her lips. "I wanted to be sure."

Lovely smiled.

"Tell you what . . . I'm tired robbing poor people for cell phones and a couple of US dollars. I have my eyes on something better."

Lovely's face lit up.

"There's this guy I suspect to be very rich," he continued. "But, I think he's hiding his possessions. I need you to get close to him . . . try to get information that can help me and my boys."

It wasn't hard to recall what had just happened. Lovely thought about the possible bruise around her neck and swallowed hard.

"Close to him?"

"You know what I mean," Junior said, frowning. "Close, but not that close."

Lovely nodded, hardly moving her head.

"In fact," Junior said, now smiling, "that job will pay for the most lavish wedding anyone have seen in Liberia. We will use the money to get married."

The power of love arose in Lovely's heart, enthused by the prospect of getting married.

"Tell me where to meet him," she said. "I'll be there before you know it."

Meeting Bashir, the rich businessman Junior had in mind, was a divine pleasure. The most important thing was how things would turn out. She would not suffer like her mother had, an old fashion woman who did not know anything about excitements in life. She wasn't going to sell potato greens at Gobachop market to make a living.

Two days later, Lovely met Bashir at the bar-room he frequented to meet beautiful women. She convinced Bashir she could not have folks over at her home because she still lives with her mother who would not approve. It would be best if she came to his place, which the man thought was a better idea. Bashir pursued women he desired with the same eagerness he used to become a very successful businessman.

As the friendship between Lovely and Bashir deepened, within a short time, so did his trust. He entrusted her with important business and personal details, including the safekeeping of his cash and other valuables. With intimate plans in mind, Bashir happily arranged Lovely's visit to his place.

There are times bad luck comes, and then you wait to see what you can make of it. But you could call it fate, like when an overtired mother who is sick of giving advice to unheeding children bring down her hand heavily on them. And, sometimes fate can be cruel.

As arranged, soon Lovely was standing in front of the massive steel gate at Bashir's home, waiting to be let in. Junior and his gang discreetly follow close behind. Bashir opened the gate, expecting his date. But to his surprise, close behind Lovely, in rushed a few men with guns, wearing hoodies.

The robbery had been executed exactly to plan. Before Bashir knew what had happened, guns were being pointed at his face. Junior fired his gun close to the man's head to show they meant business. The robbery was easy because Bashir had shared details of his home layout to Lovely, who had given it to Junior. They took the entire contents of his safe; cash, jewelry, diamonds and other precious rough stones. It would set Junior up for life.

Junior shot the man anyway.

Fate can be unstoppable too. What they had not planned for was to carry out the robbery on the same night another gang was carrying on theirs. Bashir's house was near Duport Road, where the special police unit was already responding to another armed robbery call. The police followed the sound where the latest gunshot had originated from, Bashir's house.

A dozen or so policemen waited near the gate in ambush, blocking the path where Junior and his gang would try making a quick getaway. Other than the gate, there would be quite literally no place else to leave the compound.

As soon as they reached the gate, the police called for the robbers to surrender. Junior and the gang members responded by shooting at the police officers. The policemen fired back. Instinctively, Junior grabbed Lovely's arm and pulled her in front of him, daring the law officers to shoot at a woman. With Lovely as his shield, he continued shooting at the policemen, wounding an officer. A sniper took aim at the couple, firing several quick shots. Lovely felt a sharp pain just before blocking out.

Lovely woke up to throbbing pain again, still handcuffed to the hospital bed. In and out of consciousness, she later learned Junior had not made it. He had died from his gunshot wounds. Junior had been shot in the neck and she had taken bullets in her shoulders and leg. Not only would she be facing charges for armed robbery, but it would be a long way to recovery. The bullet wound was a mess, as if she'd been hit with two different kinds of weapon at once. How could she possibly walk again?

## We Will Remember Them

In 1990, a group of armed men, members of the Armed Forces of Liberia, stormed the Lutheran Church in Sinkor, killing untold numbers of unarmed civilians. The effect one of Liberia's most notorious massacres had on one family is told from Meanyean's memory, a survivor leaving Liberia to live in Australia for good.

# We Will Remember Them

Meanyean put his hand up when the airport security guard took out a metal detector to scan his body. He could not wait to get over this part of the traveling process. Wearing his Sunday's best, a multi-colored embroidered designed shirt over a pair of slim fitted long trousers, one could tell he had put more efforts than usual. His trousers had a prominent pleat. The small backpack over his left shoulders was searched slowly and thoroughly. The security guard spoke to him in French, who did have the rough mannerisms of most African security personnel manning ubiquitous checkpoints all over the continent.

Everything seemed to be going on in blur, it was unreal. Meanyean felt extreme elation, anxiety, and uncertainty. The conflicting emotions surging through him made him feel he was in a stupor, in an unreal dream. It was simply too good to be true.

A door opened and another door opened. The humid night air hit him when he stepped out of the air-conditioned building. A long bus came rolling on the tarmac and stopped, and Meanyean and his daughter stepped onto the bus. There was a mixture of people stepping onto the bus too; rich African elites, white non-governmental workers, Lebanese businessmen, and a greenie like him.

The distance the bus traveled was relatively short, with the journey lasting for just five minutes. A cordon of uniformed security personnel stood on the side waving them forward as they searched their travel documents for the last time. Meanyean climbed onto the stairs leading up to the huge bird. He walked gingerly, uncertain of his steps as if afraid he could fall at any time. At the top of the stairs, right at the entrance of the airplane, a white lady smiled at him and said something in French, after briefly examining his ticket. She softly patted Plaser's head, Meanyean's daughter, and escorted her to her seat while pointing out where Meanyean was to sit beside her. Meanyean gazed from the airplane window, admiring the faint glow of light bickering in the distance, showing the continent he was leaving for the first time in his life. He wondered if he would see family members and friends again. This moment he had craved for so long was finally here.

"Monsieur," a blonde hair airline hostess said.

Startled, Meanyean realized he had been blocking the way forward. He strolled the narrow pathway between identical rolls of seats on both sides of him. A white man offered and put Meanyean's overhead luggage into the tight overhead compartment. This surprised him. A white man had never served him before.

Meanyean sat down, and with some efforts, fastened his seatbelt like he had been taught in IOM orientation class. Then, he helped Plaser with hers. The airplane engine roared and the wind buffeted. He could feel the aircraft picking up speed, accelerating, and then climbing far above Africa's ground. It was hard breathing in a steady rhythm. But Meanyean was more than happy to finally leave Africa and her deprivations behind. He tilted his head back, and with more efforts than expected, calmed his jitters. Before long, the dream took him back to the streets of Monrovia. It was 1990, at the Lutheran Church compound.

For one nation to control another for their selfish purpose through war is a form of barbarism. How can one make sense of the fratricidal war that reigned supreme in Liberia in the nineties? Overwhelmed with confusion, Liberia had known one successful coup and dozens of real and faked counter coups; thankfully, none of which had been successful. What worked in Liberia's favor was the coup lasted for a few hours, and within days things returned to normal. But this thing about Liberians getting guns and shooting each other because of political and ethnic differences was something entirely new. Like most people, including Meanyean, they did not know how to react.

It was 1990, and Monrovia was gripped by a complicated civil war. Across the bridge from Caldwell to St. Paul Bridge, Beer Factory, Logan Town, and all the way to Bushrod Island, Freeport, forces of a maverick rebel leader, Prince Johnson, would soon be in control. The Independent National Patriotic Front, a breakaway rebel group, battled forces of the main rebel group, the National Patriotic Front, to the North, and the Armed Forces of Liberia (AFL) loyal to President Samuel Doe. Soldiers of the INPFL were strong and disciplined, led by a notorious leader known for his quick orders of civilian executions. From the north in the suburb of Paynesville, and the Robertsfield highway, from Buchanan to ELWA Junction, and much of the rest of the country, was controlled by the National Patriotic Front of Liberia (NPFL), a ragtag band of rebels loyal to the astute, sophisticated and dubious, Charles Taylor. The soldiers of the NPFL were well-armed, wore women's wigs, and the latest fashion in jeans. This group of rebels also gained notoriety for atrocities committed against civilians.

In the city center, the prosperous eastern Sinkor suburb, and the main military barrack, BTC, were controlled by the Armed Forces of Liberia. The American trained AFL had proved inept at stopping a rebel advance from the northeast of the country. They were a brutal military force that used scorched earth policy in an attempt to stop the rebels from advancing. Summary executions and massacres of civilians became the hallmark of the national army. All warring factions were brutish, and their attitudes toward civilians, predatory.

Meanyean was a regular high school 17-year-old interested in things boys his age enjoyed. He liked listening to music, name-brand sneakers, and girls. One particular girl, Hawa Draper, stole his heart. Meanyean was deeply in love with her and made it a priority to keep up with the latest trends at Cathedral High School. He looked forward to graduating from high school and going on to the government-owned university.

Hawa Draper was the daughter of a wealthy politician and an illiterate woman from Sinje, in western Liberia. She had inherited her light complexion from her half-Lebanese grandfather on her father side. He and high-spirited Hawa planned on getting married as soon as they completed university.

Like other high school students, Meanyean and Hawa would sometimes sneak over to Monte Carlo, a betting shop, after school to gamble illegally; they were not yet 18 years old. At Monte Carlo, they simply had to take off their uniforms and put on dokafleh[1]. And to avoid any suspension, they usually bought these clothes from peddlers on the corner of Broad and Mechlin Streets.

One day state radio announced that dissidents who had crossed over to Liberia from Ivory

---

1 Used clothes sold by local vendors.

Coast had been driven back. The news seemed good, but little did people know the world would come crashing down soon. From December 1989, within six months of the commencement of the war in Nimba County, a splintered rebel movement came knocking on the gates of Monrovia, and then, things started to unravel. Paranoia became the order of the day. Government soldiers started killing mentally ill people in the streets out of fear that they could be rebel spies disguised as mentally ill people. Then, anyone wearing red-color clothing item carried the suspension of solidarity with the rebels. Any young man with a muscular body meant he had been undergoing training with the insurgents. If the young man looked thin, or wore dreadlocks, it meant he had been trawling the jungle as a rebel fighter, and did not have sufficient food to eat. Looking one way or another, one could be arrested at the mushrooming checkpoints springing up in residential neighborhoods throughout the country.

Soon enough, a death squad vigilante group sprang up. Headless bodies were discovered in the poorer sections of the city, starting in Paynesville on Pipeline Road. The whole country felt the panic and tension grew. People still carry on with daily living, like feeding their children and going to work. Miantona, Meanyean's father, was no different. He got dressed, while arguing with his wife about his safety, and went to work.

Miantona was not one of those privileged kids. He had gone to college in the United States on a government scholarship, obtaining a Masters degree. This education had afforded him a position as Assistant Minister for Curriculum Development at the Ministry of Education. He wasn't about to succumb to fear and not show up for work. He kissed his wife lightly on the cheek, meeting her nervous stare.

"Look dear," he said, trying to be convincing. "If these boys enter the city, they'll be here only a few days. Everything will get back to normal soon."

Meanyean hurriedly put his uniform on and joined his father in the small family car.

Miantona was a man of few words, but he'd become a talker on the way to work. He suggested to his son that if they're ever stopped and questioned at a checkpoint, Meanyean should escape if there was an opportunity.

"I could never leave you, Papa," Meanyean answered. "We will die together if it comes to that. Besides, God is watching over us."

"God allows innocent people to die too, Meanyean," he said. "Just promise me you won't pick up a gun. Don't fight anyone, let alone kill for religious, ethnic, or political reason."

Soon enough they reached a checkpoint at the entrance of the Gabriel Tucker Bridge from the direction of the Freeport. To their despair, modern weapons were out on display. About five soldiers wearing fishing nets over their faces, with misfit uniforms on, if you would call it uniform, appeared; fingers on the triggers and waving M-16 assault rifles dangerously. A small group of young boys, barely teens, stood to the side with their hands resting on top of their heads. Two soldiers stood before them, pointing their rifles. A few of the boys had wet spots at the front of their pants.

A soldier marched out in front of the car. Meanyean's heart sank. The soldier's combat boots crunched over the gravels, each step with military precision. He raised his AK-47 and stood central to the checkpoint, barrel down, just waiting for their terrified eyes to meet his. Then, he ordered Meanyean and his father out of the car.

"Remember what I told you," Miantona mumbled to his son.

In a strange, but lucky twist, the soldier recognized Miantona.

"You do not remember me, do you?" the soldier asked.

Miantona did not remember the man from anywhere.

"I was one of your students," the soldier said. "You were a good man. I will let you and your friend go."

Meanyean let out his breath. They got back in the car without any hassle. Miantona drove his son to Cathedral High School gate, dropped him off, and said good-bye.

That evening Miantona did not return home, nor the following evening or the next. They searched at his office, asked colleagues, visited relatives and friends; no one had seen or heard from him. Miantona had vanished that day. They wonder whether he had been killed by one of the rebels, or had been kidnapped. They weren't sure he was alive, with all the uncertainty in the city. That was the last time Meanyean saw his father or the family car.

It was becoming increasingly difficult for ordinary people to go about their normal business. People were doing their best dealing with the enforced disappearances, ethnic killings, and revenge killings. Rebels looted and continue committing atrocities against civilians. Encircling the capital, and a paranoid government, ill-disciplined, blood-thirsty armed men targeted civilians. It was becoming doubtful if schools would remain open.

The sparkle of youthful times was being extinguished; people were disappearing, even parents. Things were happening in ways the young people had not seen before. It was as if laughing was a crime. Any citizens appearing to be an emotional shade above depression were regarded as rebel supporters. Only babies laughed, and even then, it wasn't for long. Sometimes Meanyean felt like curling up in the fetal position and cry like he was a baby again. But he had to be strong for their mother who seemed to be having a mental breakdown. How had life come to this?

Through it all, Hawa was at his side. One day while they sat struggling to make sense of anything, Hawa told him how her father, who owns a few gas stations, had trouble keeping it from being looted. Her mother, too, was having a nervous breakdown. Meanyean told her that they had not yet heard from his father, and his mother was having a hard time dealing with the situation. She sat by the window hoping that her husband would show up, stays up all night hoping she would hear him and open the door quickly for him to be saved, and was beginning to fear for Meanyean's life. She was afraid her son would suffer the same fate as her husband, simply disappear like many others were.

"I wish those damn rebels had not brought their war here," Hawa said.

Meanyean reached for her hand and pulled her close to him. Her hands were sweaty.

"We could leave this madness, Meanyean," Hawa said. "We can leave Liberia and go to Sierra Leone as Maxwell and his family did. We would settle there until all this is over."

Meanyean said nothing.

"I have some money," Hawa continued. "We can make our way through Bomi Hills."

Meanyean sighed, thinking how to respond to her offer.

"Hawa, I cannot leave Liberia now," he managed to say. "I can't leave with my mother in such a condition. She's losing her mind over my father's disappearance. Besides, my younger sister is sick. We have very little money. I'm the head of the house now, with my father gone. I have to take care of my responsibilities."

"I was offering to pay for them too," Hawa said. "We were not going without them."

Meanyean forced a smile.

"That's good of you, Hawa," he said. "That's why I love you so much. You are a good person. But . . . ."

"But?"

"Being Gio, I'm a target," Meanyean said. "We are being targeted by the AFL soldiers. They will think that I'm a rebel spy, and that will put you in danger as well. Besides, my mother will never leave Monrovia. Not until she knows what happened to my father."

Hawa would wait another day to convince him, that is, if he could convince his mother. One could only hope if at least, one believes in a change of heart. Meanyean and Hawa ended the day without saying good-bye, and that was the last time he saw his beloved Hawa Draper. There were no mobile phones then, no social media, and nothing to keep in touch with a loved one, once you were separated by a physical distance in those days.

One thing constant throughout this turbulent time was the ubiquitous BBC's Focus on Africa. Rebels actually stopped fighting to listen to the program in keeping track of each other's progress. One time while Charles Taylor was being interviewed by Robin White, a government-linked death squad targeted the wrong tribe and went on the rampage that night.

How could families go forward when loved ones were being taken? Things continued to fall apart. The war tore people apart, even those who once were close as brothers. The purposes of car-ing for and supporting each other began to vanish, neighbors began turning on each other.

In war, nowhere is safe. Nowhere. It was that night Meanyean's mother made the fateful decision that the family should seek refuge in the Lutheran Church Compound in Sinkor. Liberians from all walk of life reverence and respected church, and anything that has to do with religion. Meanyean, his mother, now incoherent with grief, and his younger sister, hurried to the sprawling Lutheran church compound in Sinkor, located on Tubman Boulevard.

With rebel insurgents advancing closer to the Executive Mansion, the residence of the Liberian president, some wondered whether or not the church compound would be attacked. Most people hoped and prayed the compound would be spared, being a church ground.

Monrovia had become chaotic, law and order had broken down. People were seeking refuge in religious buildings. The Lutheran Church was not different. Every nook and cranny of the Lutheran church was filled with people; men and women, old and young, and children. The classrooms, inner rooms and the sanctuary itself became an unruly camp. The men among the displaced people, like Meanyean, took turns keeping watch at night. Even in these trying times, there were the usual boyfriend/girlfriend quarrels. People fought over where to lie down, while children cried for whatever reasons. There were problems with food, who had some and where could one go to get some. Soon the news reached them that soldiers had entered a UN compound one night and killed civilians, which brought a few days of dread. But the optimists said a church compound was sacred, and could not be attacked.

Then one night, drunken soldiers came banging on the iron gates of the church compound, issuing vile threats. The moral sanctity of the church at first seemed a deterrent to keep the soldiers. But, for how long? The next morning life continued as they were. Meanyean stayed with his mom and sister, encouraging them that things would be okay. He thought about Hawa Draper.

A night later the unthinkable unfolded like in a movie. A group of soldiers stormed into the Lutheran church. The church turned into a battlefield, as soldiers pointed their weapons and began unloading them, shooting at men, women, and children until the guns were empty. As far as the eyes could see, the wounded and dead lay all over the sanctuary floor with bright scarlet blood flowing everywhere. Then the sadistic soldiers moved from room to room, shooting, killing, and maiming people who were not yet dead, with cutlasses. When soldiers heard even a moan, they'd use machetes to chop survivors into pieces. They had lost all self-control.

Meanyean first resolved when he heard shots were to run. Earlier that evening his mother told him instead of sleeping upstairs in one of the rooms, she would be in the main church praying. That was where Meanyean ran. It would be best that the three of them die together.

When he entered the place, his agile movement seemed far too slow as bullets whistled past by. Meanyean saw his mother and sister dropping abruptly, their bodies covered in blood. Then, a sudden gush of pain jolted throughout his body; his stomach ached, his arms lost tension, and his legs began to weaken. It was almost sudden that he heard nothing anymore.

The next thing Meanyean was conscious of was the choking smell of stale gunpowder enveloped in the church. He could not remember how much time had passed. However, he recognized the lifeless bodies of his mother and sister. All around one could see stray limbs and dead people, once beautiful men, women, and children, young and old, who now was no longer recognizable as humans. White aide workers, journalists, and church bishops were first at the scene.

"Meanyean, never let the world forget our deaths," he heard his mother's voice, clear as day. "Let the world know what happened at the Lutheran church compound. But, not only that, don't forget about the other civilians massacred at Carter Camp, Harbel, Duport Road, Sinje, and elsewhere."

"I will not let the world forget, Mama."

Then, Meanyean slowly regain consciousness to the quiet voice of the pilot announcement in French, and later in French-accented English, that they would begin descending into Paris Charles De Gualle Airport.

"Monsieur?"

Meanyean slowly opened his eyes.

"We've arrived," the hostess said, smiling.
Meanyean nodded and smiled.

Eight-year-old Lydia is separated from her family during the civil war. Through her bravery and self-initiative, she endured abuse from the woman who had rescued her. Lydia never gave up. She drew pictures, sang songs and recited poems to get through the hard times. Lydia was always brave.
Paperback: 50 pages
ISBN-13: 978-1945408120
Size: 6 x 0.1 x 9 inches

The terrifying announcement on the radio about Black Cat was alarming, but 11-yr-old Gonty and his younger sister, Layeveh, had no idea what was going on. They were too busy doing what boys and girls their age do; playing with their friends or were at school. As the drama unfolded in the community, the brother-sister team witty observations and clever actions soon led to the capture of Liberia's most notorious criminal. Even the police chief was impressed, making them heroes.
Paperback: 62 pages
ISBN-13: 978-1945408328
Size: 6 x 0.1 x 9 inches